A *DISCOVER* BOOK

come to the
ocean
with me

TWO CHILDREN SPEND A DAY ENJOYING GOD'S CREATION

By Mary Carpenter Reid

Illustrated by June Goldsborough

Copyright © 1991 Augsburg Fortress
Text copyright © 1991 Mary Carpenter Reid

ISBN 0-8066-2551-1   LCCN 91-71035

Manufactured in the U.S.A.   AF 9-2551

95 94 93 92 91 1 2 3 4 5 6 7 8 9 10

AUGSBURG • MINNEAPOLIS

To precious Mallory

My cousin lives many, many miles from God's ocean.
So when my cousin came on an airplane to visit me,
I knew just what to do.

We changed into our swimsuits
and rubbed our noses with lotion.

We packed a lunch.

We took big towels from the closet.

And we found as many sand toys as we could carry.
Then, we hurried to the beach for a whole day.

I took my cousin to *see* the ocean that God made.

Ta rah!
There was—
    More water than my cousin had ever seen.
    More sand than my cousin had ever seen.
    And maybe more sky than my cousin had ever seen.

We pretended that the water and the sand
and the sky *saw* us.
They must have known that my cousin came
from many miles away,
for the water rushed here and there,
and sent its waves to wink at us.

The sand rolled out a plushy, mushy carpet
for our feet,
while the sky came from all around the world.

It reached up to the sun,
and whispered to the sun.
and the sun smiled at us.

I took my cousin to *hear* the ocean that God made.
First a lifeguard talked into a horn.
Then a baby cried.
Then a girl laughed.
But every single minute,
we could hear the ocean roaring and rumbling—
with crashing, splashing waves.

We shouted back at the noisy ocean.
We shouted louder and louder, until—maybe—
a faraway boat *heard* us.
The boat slowed and turned.
Its sails puffed.
It hurried toward us!

We ran and hid behind a giant rock.
We didn't make a sound.
And when we came out again, the boat was gone.

I took my cousin to *smell* the ocean that God made.
On the beach—
    Yummy hot dogs cooked on a fire.
    Black smoke curled up, up, and away.
    Balls and straw mats and old seaweed
    grew warm in the sun.

But those smells stayed on the beach.

At the water, there was only one smell—
the smell of the sea.

The waves came.
I think they *smelled* my cousin and me.

One rolled right up to our feet.
It sniffed our toes and ran back to its friends.

Then it took a big breath, stood tall,
and rolled right up to us again.
KER-SCOOSH!
The wave sneezed.
It sprayed all over us.
And it didn't use a tissue.

I took my cousin to *taste* the ocean that God made.
The water was wet and salty on our tongues.
But the sand had no taste.
It crunched in our teeth.

We sat on towels and ate peanut butter
and grape jelly sandwiches.
We pulled apart chocolate creme cookies
and licked away the creme.

We chewed on juicy, sour pickles
and drank bubbly soda from a can.

A shiny gray and white seagull soared
through the air.
He swooped down to the waves to catch his
lunch from the sea.

Then he landed on the beach.
He jerked and ran across the sand.
And stopped.
And jerked and ran some more, until
he came to us.

The seagull *tasted* our peanut butter and
grape jelly sandwiches.

But he shook his beak and flew back to his
lunch in the sea.

I took my cousin to *touch* the ocean that God made.

Cold, foamy, wet water tickled our hands . . .
our toes . . . our ankles . . . our knees . . .
and dotted our ribs with goosebumps.

We jumped into the waves.
Like a big washing machine, the waves rolled
us over and over, and sent us back
to the beach.

We found—
    Shells, new and crisp, with sharp, thin edges.
    Shells, so old the sea had rubbed them smooth and small,
    and tossed them away.
    Shells, closed tightly, with something living inside.

The wind blew in to play with us.

It *touched* my cousin and me.

The wind—
    Gave dancing lessons to our hair.
    Fluff-dried our shirts.
    Carried our kites high—high—high
    into the clouds.

My cousin and I left the beach when the sun
slipped down and turned everything orange.

On other days, I—
    Had *seen* the ocean.
    Had *heard* the ocean.
    Had *smelled* the ocean.
    Had *tasted* the ocean.
    Had *touched* the ocean.

But today was twice as nice as any of those
other days.
Because today—
    I *shared* God's ocean with my cousin.